Dionne Warwick
and David Freeman Wooley
Little Man

Illustrated by Fred Willingham

Charlesbridge

To my entire family: my two sons and all six of my grandchildren.

—D. W.

*It is my sincere hope that this story, based on my childhood, will inspire
other Little Men and Little Women around the world to follow their dreams.
This book is dedicated to my amazing daughters, Veda Davida and
Davina E'man Wooley. I love you. You're my "purpose."*

—D. F. W.

*To my mom and dad for supporting me while I pursued my "thing."
To my son Cassius: may God grant me the wisdom to guide you as you pursue yours.*

—F. W.

Text copyright © 2011 by Dionne Warwick and David Freeman Wooley
Illustrations copyright © 2011 by David Freeman Wooley
All rights reserved, including the right of reproduction in whole or in part in any form.
Charlesbridge and colophon are registered trademarks of Charlesbridge Publishing, Inc.

Published by Charlesbridge
85 Main Street
Watertown, MA 02472
(617) 926-0329
www.charlesbridge.com

Library of Congress Cataloging-in-Publication Data
Warwick, Dionne.
    Little Man / Dionne Warwick and David Freeman Wooley ; illustrated by Fred Willingham.
        p. cm.
    Summary: A young boy finds his passion and purpose in life—playing the drums.
    ISBN 978-1-57091-731-8 (reinforced for library use)
[1. Drum—Fiction. 2. Perseverance (Ethics)—Fiction. 3. African Americans—Fiction.]
I. Wooley, David Freeman. II. Willingham, Fred, ill. III. Title.
PZ7.W25823Li 2011
[E]—dc22   2010023523

Printed in Singapore
(hc) 10 9 8 7 6 5 4 3 2 1

Illustrations done in pastels and airbrush on Canson Mi-Teintes paper
Display type and text type set in Grilled Cheese and Adobe Garamond
Color separations by KHL Chroma Graphics, Singapore
Printed and bound April 2011 by Imago in Singapore
Production supervision by Brian G. Walker
Designed by Diane M. Earley

Everybody in my neighborhood has a thing—something they like to do more than anything else in the world. Mrs. Cruz's thing is taking care of little poodles. Mr. Johnson's thing is working on his old convertible.

And me? Well, everybody calls me Little Man, and drums are *my* thing.

The more I play the drums, the better I get to know them. That makes them kind of like friends.

BOOM. BOOM. BOOM. BOOM.
That's the big old bass drum.

Rat–a–tat–a–rat–a–tat.
The snare drum sounds like it's laughing when I hit it right.

And when I need a **ping** or a **crash,** I can always count on the cymbals.

My favorite part is putting them all together.

BOOM BOOM
rat–a–tat
ping–ping
CRASH!

One day, while I'm out getting some earplugs for my grandma, I see something amazing in Mrs. Wynn's store window—a shiny red bike!

I have got to have that bike. The guys at school with bikes do cool things like ride over to watch football games at Douglas Stadium or go to see half-price movies at the Columbus Theater on Wednesdays.

If I had that bike, I could go, too. And maybe I could use it to take some lessons at the music school across town. There's only one problem. Bikes cost a lot of money, and I don't have any.

So I babysit.

I walk dogs.

I carry grocery bags.

And I wash cars.

But after working for a whole month, I still don't have enough money for the bike.

When I'm not working, I play my drums. Sometimes my friends make fun of me because . . . well, I'm not very good yet. Even my brother says that when I play, babies cry, dogs howl, and grown-ups run away.

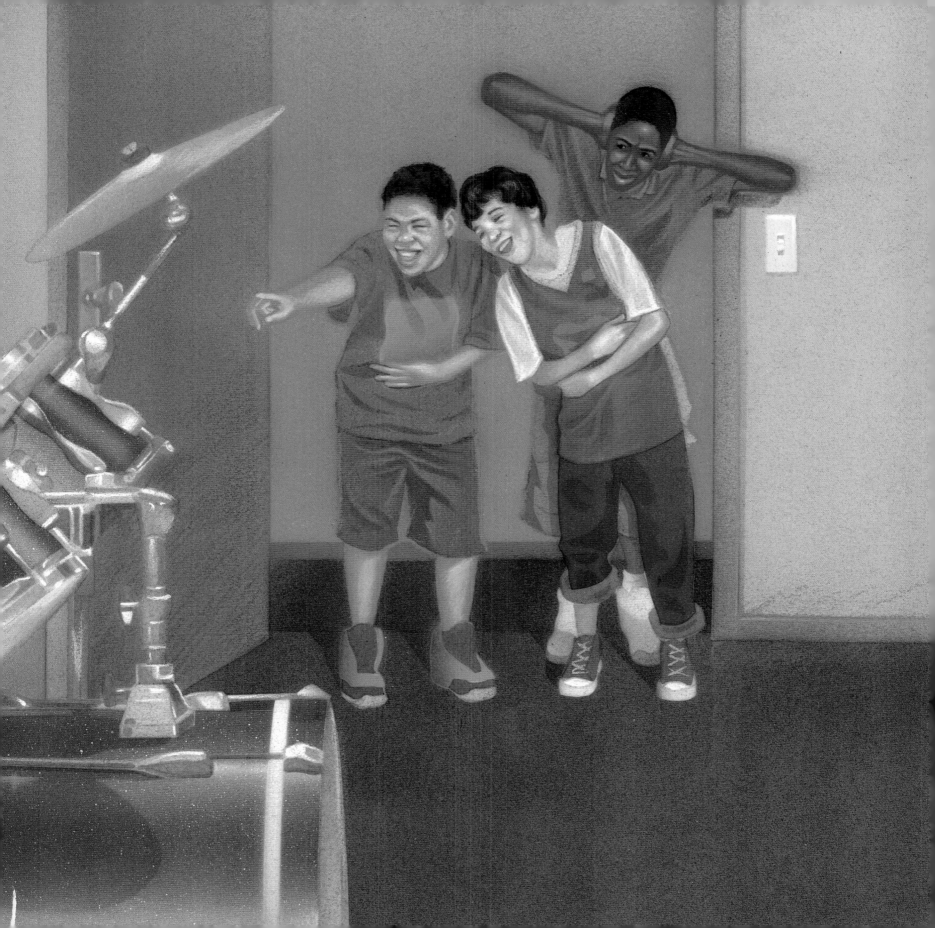

Well, I decide to have a talk with Dad.

"Dad," I say, "drums are my thing, and I want to get better."

My dad smiles at me. "Drumming is your passion," he says. "It's what your dreams are made of. You should never give up your dreams. If you follow them, you'll find your purpose."

"What purpose?" I ask.

"What you're supposed to do with your life. Just keep practicing," he says, patting me on my back.

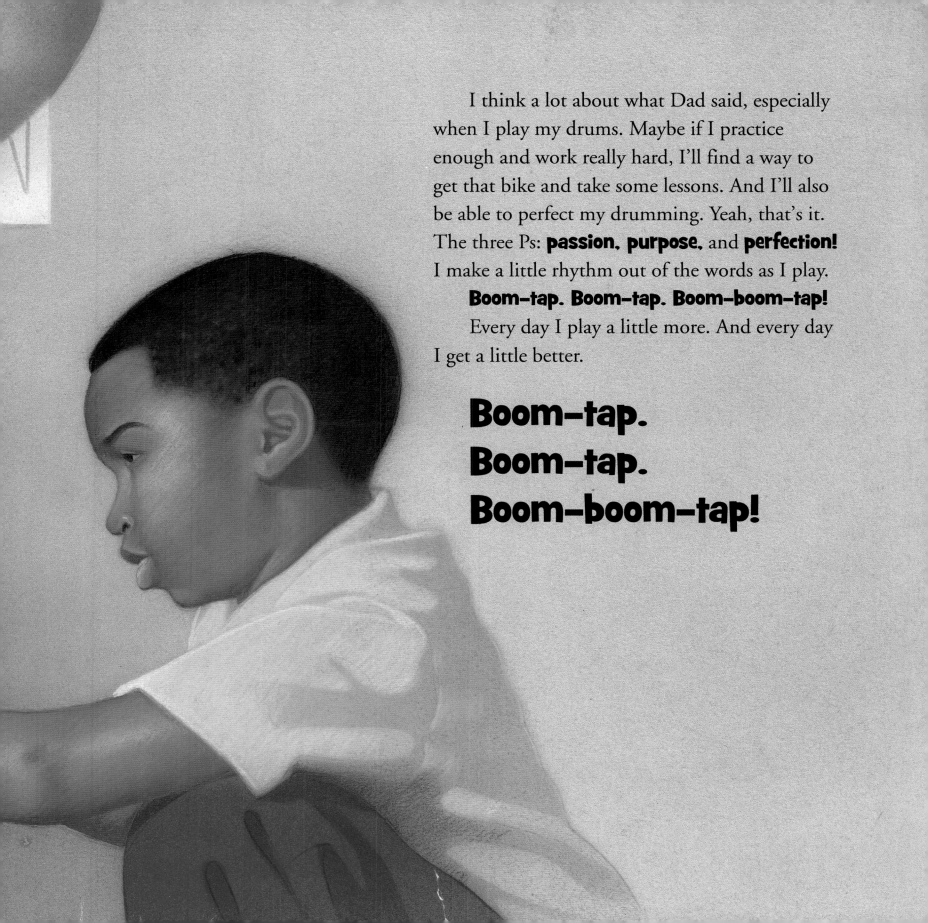

I think a lot about what Dad said, especially when I play my drums. Maybe if I practice enough and work really hard, I'll find a way to get that bike and take some lessons. And I'll also be able to perfect my drumming. Yeah, that's it. The three Ps: **passion, purpose,** and **perfection!** I make a little rhythm out of the words as I play.
Boom–tap. Boom–tap. Boom–boom–tap!
Every day I play a little more. And every day I get a little better.

Boom–tap.
Boom–tap.
Boom–boom–tap!

My friends stop making fun of me. One day they
knock on my window. "Little Man, open up!" they yell.
"We want to dance to that neat beat!"

One of my friends stops dancing long enough to say,
"Hey, Little Man, you should play for the block party later
next month. Mr. Johnson's organizing it."

"*Me?* Play drums at the block party? No way," I say.
But later that night I just can't stop thinking about it.

The next morning the block party is still on my
mind. If I want to stop thinking about it, I have to do
something. So I ask Mr. Johnson, "Can I do my thing?"
He says yes!

The block party is only three weeks away, so I don't have a lot of time to get ready. I practice and think about the three Ps.

Boom–tap.

Boom–tap.

Boom–boom–tap.

Then the big day arrives. The whole neighborhood comes to the block party. Mr. Marco grills up hot dogs and sausages from his grocery store, and Mrs. Marco serves ice-cream cones. But I'm too nervous to eat a single bite.

Mr. Johnson climbs onto a platform and holds up his hands. Everybody gathers around to hear.

"Ladies and gentlemen, we have a special treat today," he announces. "Little Man is going to play his drums for us!"

I walk onto the platform. My heart is pounding in my chest. But when I see my drums, I don't feel nervous anymore. I'm ready to do my thing.

Boom-tap! Boom-tap! Boom-boom-tap!

I look up and see something amazing.
The whole block is rocking out to my
rhythms, dancing to my drums. It's like magic.

When I finish playing, everybody claps and cheers,
and I'm so proud. And I can't believe what happens next—
Mr. Johnson takes off his hat and passes it around the crowd.
People put money in it—money for me, because they like
my music!

After the party I count the money I earned from playing
the drums and working all summer.

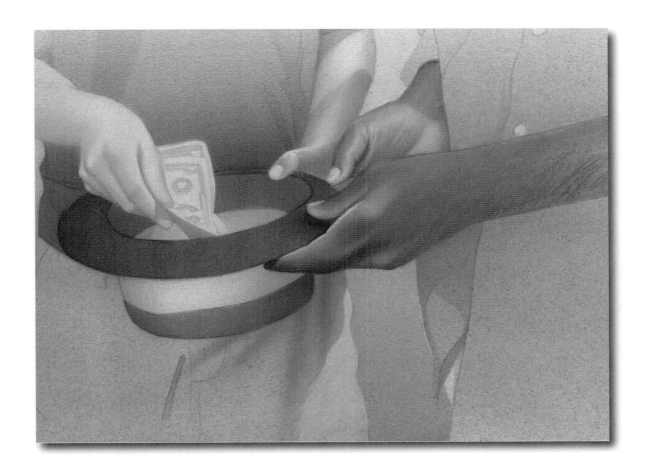

I have just enough to buy that bike. Now I can get those lessons!

I'm Little Man—and drums are my thing. What's yours?